BORN FROM FIRE

TALES FROM THE LONGVIEW #1

HOLLY LISLE

Published by OneMoreWord Books

Tales from the Longview, Episode 1: Born from Fire

SECOND EDITION

Cover Design: Holly Lisle

Cover Art: © 3000AD, BigStockPhoto.com

Holly's Author Photo: © Holly Lisle

Copyright © 2014, 2017 by Holly Lisle

Content Editor: Matthew Turano

Copy Editor: SilverJayMedia.com

This story was originally released as Enter the Death Circus

PUBLISHER'S NOTICE

This is a work of fiction. Seriously. Resemblances to real characters, real solar systems, real spaceships, and real faster-than-light travel are entirely coincidental. Names, characters, places, and tech are products of the author's imagination, and any brilliant guy who appears halfway through the story is not your cousin Bob, no matter how much he insists otherwise.

Print ISBN-13: 978-1-62456-026-2

Kindle ISBN-13: 978-1-62456-025-5

For Matthew

CATCHING UP?

The TALES FROM THE LONGVIEW Series Overview

Inhabited by a crew of misfits fleeing nightmare pasts, with a cargo of Condemned slated to die at the hands of the highest bidders, and with a passenger roster made up exclusively of people *not* who they claim to be, *The Longview* serves the hidden agenda of an eccentric recluse bent on playing puppet master to all of Settled Space.

IN THIS EPISODE 1: Born From Fire (originally *Enter the Death Circus*)

When love is crime, who will save the guilty?

After falling in love and fathering a child, a young criminal refuses to voluntarily throw himself into a lake of fire to gain his community's forgiveness. So he's sentenced to death and sold to the owner of a spaceship that buys criminals like him. But the ship and its crew are not quite what they appear to be.

NEXT IN EPISODE 2: The Selling of Suzee Delight

When slavery is virtue, who will fight for vice?

When Suzee Delight, famous Cheegoth courtesan, murders the five most powerful Pact Worlds' Administrators during a private summit, the owner of *The Longview* Death Circus struggles against conspiracy to win the bidding for her execution. Meanwhile, Suzee's powerless supporters race to save her, while the leaders of worlds pull strings to guarantee her death.

IN EPISODE 3: The Philosopher Gambit

When the mighty are monsters, what will monsters become?

An exiled philosopher buys a pretty girl a dress for her execution, by doing so becoming a hunted, wanted man with a death sentence on his own head and killers on his trail. The secretive owner of *The Longview* intervenes, putting his crew in harm's way to bring the condemned into his inner circle — but the hunters are close behind.

EPISODE 4: Gunslinger Moon

When freedom is silenced, who speaks for it?

Ex-PHTF slave WE-39R (This Criminal, from *Episode 1*), renamed Jex, is part of a team the Longview's Owner has tasked with finding the meaning behind Bashtyk Nokyd's enigmatic final diagram. Drawing the most undesirable assignment, Jex and an unlikely ally fight their way to pieces of the truth.

IN EPISODE 5: Vipers' Nest

When betrayal comes home, where does home hide?

With no place to run and their complete and utter annihilation the enemy's only objective, Bailey's Irish Station and the *Longview's* crew stand together against the onslaught of enemies visible and hidden.

.

CONCLUDING IN EPISODE 6

With the lies revealed, what future remains?

The location of the City of Furies is discovered, Shay has to choose between the Owner and Melie, and the path to freeing Settled Space and protecting everything that matters falls on those who never sought the task.

CHAPTER ONE

This Criminal

Down the darkness, down the line of standing cells, three words rippled urgently and under breath. "Death Circus here!"

In the dark, this criminal had waited long and longer for death to come. This criminal could not lie down, could not sit down—its captors had made certain its cell, and the cells of the others like it, permitted only standing.

With its bandaged knees pressed into one corner, its spine jammed into the other, this criminal drifted in that lightless place, never certain whether it was waking or dreaming. When it ate, it ate maggots. When it dreamed of eating, it dreamed of maggots. When it pissed or shit, it pissed or shit down its legs. When it dreamed, it dreamed of the same.

In one thing only this criminal knew a dream was a dream, and that was when it touched We-42K again, or saw its wondrous smile.

That could only be a dream, for We-Above had taken

this criminal out of its cell to watch beautiful We-42K volunteer its death and the death of the unlicensed-but-born that We-42K and this criminal had made. We-42K had stood above the flames of Return to Citizenship with the born in its arms, and had turned to smile at this criminal. It looked thin and starved and filthy standing there, and the born looked dead, and as if it had been dead for a while.

The born had been beautiful when this criminal had first seen it, when this criminal and We-42K had hidden in the hills and held each other at night, had accidentally made the born, had brought it into the world together. The born had the bright red hair of We-42k, and eyes that looked at this criminal with strange knowing—and this criminal had thought for a little while that life could hold more than work and duty.

That ended, and after the end, the capture, the sentencing, the imprisonment, this criminal watched the flames and knew that the We are right to say Only Death Forgives.

This criminal has no right of judgement, but this criminal will never forgive.

The We asked this criminal if it would volunteer for redemption as We-42K had done. This criminal spit in the face of We. It refused forgiveness and Return to Citizenship —though it cannot say why—and thus it has been judged Willful, and sentenced to Death Without Citizenship, Redemption, or Merit.

And now that death has come.

"Death Circus here!" this criminal whispers down the line.

The metal doors bang open, and light trickles down the corridor. This criminal hears the first cells at the front opening, and the thwack of the prod on naked flesh, a sound this criminal knows well, a touch it feels often.

"We offer last chance to volunteer for Return to Citizenship. Will the nameless willful thing repent?"

"It will not," the Willful at the head of the corridor rasps. This criminal thinks it recognizes that voice, unheard above a whisper before now, and it is encouraged. It puts a face to the voice and sees another like itself, another that once thought life might be made better. That Willful held strong. This criminal will be able to hold strong too, will be able to face the unknown death rather than accept the known one.

Both We say, "Then it goes to the Death Circus now."

This criminal cannot say why the Death Circus seems better than the Return to Citizenship, with its quick leap into the lake of fire.

But an unknown, unvolunteered death is a better death. This criminal has had little more to think about than that question since the immolation of We-42K and the born.

The cells open and close, the Willful, the Blasphemers, and the Infidels make their choices to volunteer death or to take death by force, and at last this criminal's cell opens, and the We stand there and drag it out into the corridor and say, "We offer last chance to volunteer for Return to Citizenship. Will the nameless willful thing repent?"

This criminal spits into the face of the guard that asks, and takes its beating, and is surprised that the beating is so light.

Then it remembers that the Death Circus buys its creatures, and that it once heard whispers of guards sentenced for Willfulness for damaging criminals so badly the Death Circus refused to pay the Tithe to the We to acquire them.

Inside, this criminal laughs just a little, and tries to work up enough fluid to spit into the face of the other guard.

Kagen

Kagen, sitting in the Verimeter desk beneath the flapping cloth of the red-and-black Death Circus tent, muttered, "I hate this filthy little moon."

Burke looked over at him and raised an eyebrow. Burke would be doing disease screening—testing blood and saliva—on every criminal offered to the Death Circus, which meant he had to get within arm's reach of the strange mixture of people sentenced to death by the owners of Fair Bluff. The town was regional center for the half-dozen settlements on The People's Home of Truth and Fairness 14-B, so it was the contact point for all Death Circuses.

"Why do you hate this moon? It looks normal enough to me."

Burke was new. Provisional Crew Three. If he could get through this screening without going to pieces, he would be permitted to take the final portion of the Provisional Crew Three entrance exam and he'd earn a paid place at the bottom rung of the *Longview's* crew, as Three Green.

Kagen had been Crew Three for just under four years, and in that time had pushed through four promotions to reach Crew Three Gold. He held the record for fastest time and most grades skipped to reach Three Gold.

He'd already taken his Crew Two entry levels. Had already achieved all of his promotion points to reach Crew Two. He had his future planned, his goal set.

He hadn't received word that he'd passed the exam, yet, but if he had—and if he could rise to Crew Two, it meant more than just the possibility of a bigger, quieter room away from the engine noise to him. It meant better pay—he'd save every extra rucet, just as he'd saved everything he'd made in the last few years.

And it meant keeping The Dream alive. There were no accelerated promotions in Crew Two, but he was sure he could still make an impression. He *had* to make an impression.

There were rumors of a promotion at the top. Unsubstantiated, but plausible.

Had been for weeks, which was what had pushed him to take the Crew Two entry levels. He wanted to be ready when opportunity arose.

Burke, Kagen thought, looked to be a slow riser. The man had only cursory interest in what he was doing. To Kagen he seemed flat and bland and far too slow. Kagen suspected Burke hadn't hurt enough to see the opportunity provided by the *Longview*, that he wasn't hungry enough to ever rise past the automatic promotions in Crew Three.

Kagen, though, had been hungry all his life.

"If there is such a thing as pure evil, it lives here," Kagen muttered.

Burke said, "How is this worse than any other Pact world?"

Kagen looked around the still-empty tent and said, "This is a PHTF franchise. If you have thirty million rucets and want to be a god, you too can own a People's Home of Truth and Fairness settlement on your own little moon. There are a couple hundred of them now, I think, and they all run on the same rules. I come from PHTF-36. I still have nightmares." And he laughed.

To show that he was over it.

Burke glanced over at him with an expression Kagen saw as bovine curiosity. "How did you get out?"

"The We sentenced me to exile in the Needle, with the reminder that I could jump at any time and be forgiven for my crime."

"You were a Mule?"

Kagen forced a grin. "Indeed. I kissed a girl, and gave her a nickname. My Sentence was Willful and Blasphemer, but I hadn't done quite enough for the Speakers for We to put me in prison. Being a Mule exiled in the Needle is supposed to be the same outcome as if you're sentenced to death... but because of the *Longview*, you know how that is." Kagen tipped his head up to the invisible point of the Needle, where the *Longview* was currently docked. "Since I didn't end up dying for my crime, it was worth it."

Burke nodded. "The secret rooms."

The rooms in the Needles were only secret to those who despised the technology that created them and the men they'd had to hire to build them. All Needles required someone to work in the top, to greet the spaceships making their rounds through their routes, to accept or reject docking.

The PHTF worlds chose to send lone criminals into exile in the Needles. Those they didn't deem valuable enough to sell to the visiting Death Circuses, anyway.

Which was what brought Kagen to this world he despised so much. Kagen, Burke, and the rest of the ground team from the *Longview* were set up to start screening candidates for purchase by the Death Circus.

The We were supposed to have had their criminals in front of the tent an hour ago, but as usual they'd managed to get a string of last-minute conversions from the ranks of the criminals sentenced to death, and the We of the People's Home of Truth and Fairness 14-B were busy burning them —or rather, having the criminals burn themselves—out back of the tent in their nasty little lake of fire.

Every PHTF world had a lake of fire, and they all

looked the same. Kagen suspected it was part of the franchise.

Kagen could hear the announcement of the crimes of the volunteers: Willfulness, Blasphemy, Infidelity, over and over. Could hear the screams as the sentenced threw themselves into the flames rather than meet their fate with the Death Circus. Charlie, who was not a member of the crew but a mandatory passenger, was doing her duty in her role as official Pact Covenant observer. She was out in back testing all the volunteers to make sure none had been drugged, and that none were forced to jump into the lake.

Because she had gone renegade, Charlie would also watch for, and enforce removal of, anyone who gave any sign whatsoever of having second thoughts.

Nineteen out of every twenty prisoners on a PHTF world would fling themselves into the lake of fire and die in agony rather than allow themselves to be purchased by a Death Circus.

So the smell of burning human flesh was strong in the tent, and the intermittent sounds of screaming were loud. Equally horrible was the cheering of the throng of observers pulled from their work and made to chant, "You're forgiven! Welcome home!" as each volunteer stopped screaming.

For an instant, Kagen was back among them. Pressed up against the fence, feeling the stares of the Speakers for We focused on him and the others with him, he cheered and screamed with the rest as the pretty young woman, sentenced for the crimes of Property of Beauty and Apart of Love, threw herself into the fire. Kagen had not been the only boy who had kept his face forward so the guards could not see the tears streaming down his cheeks as he watched her die.

Not cheering was a sign of being Apart. Everyone

cheered, because Speakers for We would note those who did not, and would investigate them for other crimes.

Each did what All did, or Each found itself locked away beneath the earth, or burning in the lake of Return to Citizenship.

He shuddered and was back in the red-and-black tent, back in someone else's horrible little world.

At last the We ran out of volunteers, and the sound of marching feet approached the tent flap of the Death Circus. Those prisoners ineligible for volunteering to repent—the murderers, rapists, pedophiles, and thieves—would come in first. They were Pact World Class A prisoners, meaning their sentencing and treatment fell within the Pact World Convention guidelines. They would be clean, well fed, well rested, and clothed, because if they weren't, The People's Home of Truth and Fairness 14-B would lose its charter, and with it the steady infusion of licensed charter world grant money from the Pact Worlds Equalization of Opportunity Committee that kept it alive. Once the Class A prisoners had been tested for diseases, Verilized, and categorized by health to determine the price the Death Circus had to pay for them, they would present their paperwork to the Death Circus judge, who would decide whether they were guilty or innocent—and would then determine whether they would be taken aboard the *Longview,* or left behind.

The Longview had to accept and purchase at least 33% Class A prisoners from those prisoners presented by the worlds it serviced in order to keep its Death Circus license.

Class B prisoners were sentenced under local jurisdiction, for anything considered a crime on that world, but not necessarily held to be a crime elsewhere. Because they were still covered by the Pact World Covenants, which ruled that no member world could carry out a death sentence, they could not be executed.

But the Pact World Covenants charter for Death Circuses was that any prisoner taken aboard a Death Circus ship must have a death sentence carried out, but only outside the Pact World borders.

It was up to the discretion of ship owners and ship captains on how these sentences would be carried out, but they had to be carried out, because each world that handed over a prisoner to the Death Circus had a written guarantee that the prisoner would die in a timely and appropriate fashion.

Class B prisoners were almost always criminals of a political or religious nature. And they always arrived at the Death Circus barely breathing: starved, caked in their own excrement, covered in sores. The only rules for Pact World members regarding Class B prisoners was that they could not be allowed to die while imprisoned, and that they had to be able to walk to and through the Death Circus under their own power.

The *Longview* crew had additional rules. The owner of the *Longview* insisted that each Class B must be showered until clean and dressed in fresh, dry, disposable clothing before entering the Death Circus tent. Nor were the PHTF guards permitted to do the washing. Members of the Death Circus crew were to do it, gently and with good soap and soft towels.

Kagen suspected the owner, whom he had never met or even been permitted to discuss, had once been a Class B prisoner on a PHTF world—one who had escaped, and who had then vowed to somehow help those still trapped.

It was a romantic notion, and considering the vast expenses of running a Death Circus, and the equally vast profits to be made for running one well, it was probably a silly one.

Nevertheless, he held that possibility as his truth until proven wrong, and occasionally assigned himself to prisoner cleanup duty. It was good for his unit's morale to see him do so, and it reminded him that, though he had escaped *his* PHTF home, many still remained.

CHAPTER TWO

This Criminal

T wo Evils from the Death Circus wash this criminal in warm, falling water, and are not unkind. They use soft cloths and something that froths white and bubbly as they rub it over this criminal's broken skin, and the white substance numbs the places where it hurts. Where its skin bleeds, they spray a bitter-smelling substance that closes the wound. This criminal wonders at the Evils that do kindness before killing.

This criminal finds the process of its death at the hands of the Evils increasingly less alarming. It listens to them talk together, easily, in terms it does not understand. As they talk, they laugh, and do not look over their shoulders to see if they have been overheard.

It thinks if it must die today, it would rather die at the hands of these.

They are Apart. Not We. They do not carry the mandatory posture of *Submission to Duty* in their backs and shoulders. They do not have the cautious speech or wary eyes of

We Report Or Are Reported. They act in a fashion this criminal can barely comprehend—they carry themselves as this criminal did when it was Apart secretly with We-42K, except without the constant fear.

Fear justified, in fact, for We-42K finally reminded itself of the requirements of *Submission to Duty* and *We Report Or Are Reported,* and brought this criminal's time with it to an end. It rejoined the We in death by choice.

This criminal cannot choose death.

> *Duty is life.*
> *Life is dying.*
> *Dying is duty.*

THAT IS part of the *Truth of We.* It is the *Truth* this criminal failed in its every thought, in its every dream, in its every waking moment.

This criminal dared to imagine some other better truth might appear. That was its first and worst crime.

On this, the day of its death, this criminal thinks somewhere else must exist, where people stand with shoulders and backs straight, with eyes forward, where they laugh aloud and don't look around to see who might have heard. This criminal thinks in the place that gave these Evils birth, a different truth already lives.

When all are washed, this criminal is led to the front of the tent with the other criminals. It can read the sign painted above the flap:

Welcome to the Death Circus
Enter and be judged.

THIS CRIMINAL AND all with it have already been judged and sentenced. All that remains, it thinks, is the form its death will take.

"We who are about to die enter the Death Circus," this criminal murmurs, and realize it has committed Blasphemy by naming itself We.

That is another crime for which it will never be charged or sentenced. This criminal can only die once.

It laughs and steps through the tent flaps.

The tent is not filled with torture devices, with spears or knives, with huge Evils crouched over criminals, ripping out the insides of their still-living victims with their filed teeth. The stories are lies, then. The tent contains a mesh-sided walkway with one-way gates that will fit Each Apart singly. When Each steps forward, a handless touch at the back pushes all forward. The gates swing open. The gates snap closed. This criminal stands always alone, as fits the nature of its crime.

But this criminal sees that not Each Apart bears scars. The criminals far in the front of the line are all healthy and well-fed and dry. And clothed in a blue version of the clothes worn by the We. Those in front of this criminal, as well as all those behind it, are gaunt and beaten and dripping from being cleaned, and they are dressed in the clothes of the Evils. Otherwise they would have been naked.

Each Apart moves through the walkway—a step, a

pause, a step, a pause—and then this criminal stands before the first of the Evils. The Evil presses something white and smooth against the arm of this criminal and holds it in place for an instant.

"No diseases," the Evil says, and marks something on a white, rectangular sheet. The texture of the sheet is exquisitely smooth, its color is unblemished. This criminal recognizes the markings on the sheet as words, though they are not words from the *Truth of We*. The evil holds the sheet out and this criminal takes the sheet and holds it carefully, and the line moves again.

"Paper," the one at the next station demands. This criminal has seen all criminals before it pass the white sheet through the small opening in the mesh. It passes its sheet through.

"Hand through the opening, hold this ball."

The ball is smooth and gray, strangely cold, slightly damp. Holding it makes pulling this criminal's flesh back through the opening impossible.

This criminal finds holding the ball and having its hand trapped in the grate uncomfortable and frightening.

"You are accused of the crime of Willfulness, with the specific charges of being alone; of sharing aloneness with another; of making an unlicensed infant; and of failure to volunteer to rejoin the We. Are you guilty?"

This criminal glares at the Evil, and says, "Yes." The ball in its hand glows the yellow-gold of summer sunlight.

The Evil looks from the ball in this criminal's hand to its face, and smiles. "Good for you. Is the other who shared your crimes here?"

This criminal does not understand the smile or the words that accompany them. This criminal has heard mockery before—if the Evil mocked, the Evil did it wrong.

This criminal says, "The unlicensed born died. We-42K volunteered to rejoin the We in Return to Citizenship."

The smile leaves the face of the Evil, and the Evil shakes its head. "I'm sorry. Truly."

"Why? This criminal is guilty. We-42K did what the We say is right."

"Do you think the We is right?"

"This criminal does not know 'you.' This criminal does not believe the *Truth of We*. But that is because this criminal is criminal. It is broken and evil. It thinks Apart, it thinks Willful, it denied We in word and deed. When it was We..."

This criminal begins to cry, then forces itself to stop.

"When it was We, it called itself We-39R, and even then, it knew it was lying."

The Evil stands up and stares into this criminal's eyes. The Evil's skin sheens with sweat, and its expression is fierce. "I was once We. Things change."

It marks the criminal's paper and adds a second sheet, hands both through the grate, and sends this criminal to the next station.

This criminal, Apart and Alone, walks forward—step, gate, step, gate—and sometimes the line pauses, and this criminal turns to look back, and sees the Evil that was once We talking to another criminal.

I was once We. Things change.

This criminal cannot get those words out of its mind. There is We, or there is death.

Things change.

The Evil was We, but it lives.

The final gate, and the final Evil, stand at last before this criminal.

The final Evil takes the papers, reads through them, and

says, "Your sentence of death is complete. Go to Door B. Stand on the identity plate. The door will open for you. Walk forward, go through the door at the back, step through the next door, turn to your right, walk through the paddock, and stand in the corral with the others who have been sentenced.

"You have been purchased by the Death Circus."

Kagen

The *Longview* ground team had already packed the Death Circus tent, and all the team members were waiting beside the landing pad for the last two shuttles. The final shuttle would pack the tent back to the hold.

Before it returned, the shuttle Kagen and Burke waited for would remove the last of the Condemned.

The Condemned stood in the corral. Each of them waited in a separate gated control cell within the corral—the last twenty-two men of a haul of over two hundred. Darkness had come, and the We who had shouted curses through the fencing at the Condemned and the Evil, as well as the guards and Speakers for We who had kept them shouting, were gone. In worlds lit only by fire, darkness brought monsters, but chased away mobs.

The quiet around the landing pad was a pleasant reprieve from the grim work of the day, and Kagen was enjoying the silence.

But Burke, who was new, wanted to talk. "No women. Why do we have no women Condemned?"

Kagen said, "PHTF settlements almost never sell off women. Any place where people live beneath the *Truth of We,* young women go to the breeding factories as soon as they're fertile. Once they lose their fertility, women can claim guilt for taking pleasure in their work in the breeding factory, and volunteer to throw themselves into the fires of Return to Citizenship, or if they swear they took no pleasure, they can volunteer for the Room of Release."

"Which is...?"

Kagen shuddered. He closed his eyes and was back where he was born, on the last day of his freedom, where he and five other older boys—he guessed he'd been about fifteen at the time—were tasked with stocking the Room of Release.

The first woman who came through was one he recognized, though she did not appear to remember him. She had been kind to him when he was small. Had sought him out, had smiled at him. She had not seemed terribly old when he was young, but a decade had aged her terribly. Her belly and breasts sagged, her face was etched with pain, and her body was scarred from repeated beatings. She looked at the boys who led her into the room and connected the chain on the floor to the collar around her neck and locked it as they had been instructed to do. She looked at them, but she didn't seem to see them.

The boys went to stand in the hall beside the door, and a line of twenty men filed into the room.

Kagen told Burke, "They're chained to the floor, alone, and packs of men who are not permitted to touch women at any other time are sent in together to Release themselves. The men are told they are experiencing the Filth of Apart, and that they must all stay together and do whatever they have to do together, so the Filth of Apart will not destroy them. What they do together is horrible."

Burke frowned. "That's not right."

"No. It isn't. When the first woman in the Room of Release dies, or when she starts screaming that she wants to

Return to Citizenship, Speakers for We drag her out and throw her into the fires—alive, dying, or dead—and a group of boys not old enough to be required to Release chain a new volunteer in her place."

The morning after he'd finished his first day working in the Room of Release, he decided he would never do that again. During the recitation of the *Truth of We,* he'd looked over at the pretty girl who always stood next to him, at whom he had never directly looked before, because looking at girls and women was something the Apart did. She was a tall, slender girl with pale skin and dark, curling hair. He leaned over and pressed his mouth to her mouth, which one of the men in the Room of Release had done when he saw one of the volunteers. And he called her "Love," as that man had done before the Speakers dragged him away.

And one of the Speakers for We saw him do it, and two guards dragged him to the House of Fairness right then.

The advantage of living on a Pact World was that the Speaker didn't kill him right there.

His sentence, handed down minutes after that single kiss, however, and directly from the Speaker for We who'd heard him say it, had exiled Kagen to the Needle on his world to serve as a cargo slave. He was to live alone in the Needle, transporting cargo from spaceships docking at the Needle to the surface. He was to do this until he died.

If the Needle worked the way the Speakers of We believed, he would have been up there with only the small supply of water and food with which they'd exiled him.

His options, when he ran out of water and food, were to volunteer to die of thirst or starvation, or to volunteer to throw himself out the airlock.

It was only because the Needles did *not* work the way

Speakers for We believed that Kagen breathed as a free man.

Burke said, "Rooms of Release. That's rough. There are rooms a lot like that on the Pact pleasure worlds. I ended up in one when I ran up a gambling debt I couldn't pay on Cheegoth. I was sentenced to work there until I had paid off my debt plus the interest—and the way it was set up, I would have never made enough money to pay off the interest. If I hadn't pissed off one of the establishment's clients and gotten myself dumped into the Indigent Lockup for the next passing ship to haul off, I would have been in there until I died or some client killed me. Cheegoth doesn't have any fairness, or any *Truth of We* to protect people."

Kagen looked at him sidelong. "Fairness isn't justice. Fairness is making a pretty girl volunteer to step into a lake of fire because not everyone else can be as pretty as she is. And there is no *truth* in the *Truth of We.* "

Burke shrugged. "What is it?"

Leaning against the temporary shuttle gate, Kagen once again felt the cold dark before dawn, when shivering and hungry, shoeless and wearing his light cotton uniform, in rain or snow or blistering heat, he'd recited the Words with every other man, woman, and child in his block.

"We speak the Truth, and the Truth speaks Us," Kagen said, keeping his voice low.
"We live by the covenants, We abide by the Words."

NEVERTHELESS, more than Burke heard him. Unbreathing silence fell behind him. The Condemned had stopped their pacing and nervous fidgeting to stare at him, bodies frozen and faces suddenly slack with animal fear. The hope that had been in all their eyes before—hope for a chance of escape, or for a chance to fight, or just for a chance at a quick, merciful death—vanished with those two soft lines.

Kagen kept going, though. He wanted Burke to understand.

> *"That none may laugh until All can laugh,*
> *That All sleep on dirt until none sleep on dirt.*
>
> *Dirt is Our birthright. Hardship is Our glory.*
> *Hardship strengthens Us. Hunger feeds Us.*
>
> *The Known is All. The new is Willful.*
> *Welcome Pain. Pain is Knowledge. We are WE."*

HE REALIZED the men in the line were whispering the Words with him. He turned and snarled, "Stop it. Now. You are not We. You're men, and every single one of you will face the justice and the death you *earned.*"

He turned to look at Burke again, and continued,

> *"Self is selfish. One is none.*
> *All are All. We are We.*
>
> *Each flesh belongs to All.*
> *Each thought belongs to All.*

Children are duty. All tend All.
Duty is life. Life is dying. Dying is duty.
We die for Duty. We are WE.

Within Each hides Evil. Be All, not Each.
In Aloneness is Willfulness. We will never be Alone.

We share, We do not own.
Property is an abomination.

Beauty is property. Property is crime.
Passion is property. Property is crime.

Love is property. We out love and lovers.
Secrets are property. We out secrets and secret-keepers.

All is Sharing. Sharing is Duty.
We serve Sharing. We are WE.

We speak the Truth, and the Truth speaks Us.
We live by the covenants, We abide by the Words.
The Will of All is all of Will. We are WE.

BURKE STOOD THERE FROWNING when Kagen finished. "None can laugh until everyone can laugh? Hunger feeds us? Beauty is crime? What sort of shit is that?"

"That's the *Truth of We.* If you laugh, you're a criminal. If you want a single thing for yourself, you're a criminal. The instant you realize you are not the same as everyone else—that you're thinking your own thoughts inside your own head—you are a criminal.

"And because sooner or later everyone realizes the thoughts in their heads belong to them, every single person in every single settlement is a criminal. And the Speakers for We, who do not live under the *Truth of We,* are the biggest criminals of all. They buy these marginal worlds and grubby moons and the franchise constitutions that make them PHTFs, and send out advertisements for new settlers to get a better life, all expenses paid."

Burke was staring at him. "How can these worlds be legal?"

"The same way the world you were on was legal. As long as the people in charge of these worlds don't ever try to claim the right that they can execute someone on a Pact world, or kill any registered citizen intentionally, they can do anything they want."

CHAPTER THREE

_____

This Criminal

The sky ship drops toward this criminal, silent. Speakers say the burning flesh of the Apart feed it, which may be true, but nothing else the Speakers say has proven true.

No. This criminal lies. *Truth of We* said this criminal would be sold to the Death Circus, which must guarantee that each criminal it purchases will have the Sentence of Death carried out. This criminal was sold. Death will come now.

Still, the ship touches the ground, noiseless. The ship does not smell of burning flesh, which is a smell that will haunt this criminal until his last thought. This criminal tries to find comfort in the absence of a scent.

In the darkness, in the silence, this criminal stands shivering, for no matter how the Evils do not seem cruel, the ship has arrived, and life now ends.

This criminal thinks—which is its first crime—of what life might have been if We-42K had remained criminal. If it had not brought the Speakers and the Guards to the hiding place. This criminal imagines a life without *Truth of We*.

But if such life exists, it will not exist for this Apart.

The sky ship's doors are open, and the line moves. The unseen hands behind push Each Apart through the tall wire corral, into the next gate.

The first criminal steps through the gates, up into the ship. The Apart does not run.

This criminal thinks when it steps through the gates, it will run. It is not ready for Death.

There is no sound as the ship doors close behind the first Apart. Just a moment later, the doors re-open and the Apart is gone. It was big, tall and strong-looking, clean and fierce, and it had shouted anger at the Evils when it waited.

The Evils have a quiet Death. It is not like the death of Return to Citizenship, which is screaming and writhing, body arcing long, then curling inward, arms and legs twisting, with skin peeling away from flesh, with flesh peeling away from bone, with bone blackening until it bursts into flame and at last is gone.

The quiet Death may be quick.

But this criminal wants to live.

The line moves too quickly. Each Apart moves forward without resistance, steps up to the ship and through the doors and is gone.

Each Apart, and then this criminal is two places away from the final corral, and it feels a sharp, quick, bright pain in its arm, and looks to see a tiny ice dart melting into its flesh.

And all its fear goes, and its anger, and its desire to live. The face of We-42K fades, and the solemn gaze of the born disappears. This criminal is washed empty inside, and steps up into Death.

Kagen

Kagen and Burke lifted the last body into its private suspended-animation unit and sealed the unit.

Kagen said, "You do the paperwork this time."

Burke nodded, took the papers from Kagen, and started to shove them into the unit's feeder slot.

Kagen said, "You weren't watching what I did. *Learn to watch.* If my head didn't already hurt, I'd have let you put them in that way. And then I'd have let you deal with the alarm and trying to get the papers sorted out on your own. Because you've watched me do twenty of those, but you evidently didn't see a thing."

Burke said, "What did I do wrong?"

"The sheets go in numerical order, print side up, all facing the same direction. If you put them in any other way, the unit alarm goes off loud enough to wake the dead."

"Why? I don't even understand why we use paper," Burke grumbled. "This whole process could be shortened to minutes with a single data thread."

"Paper can't disappear when a unit shorts," Kagen said, "and the hermetically sealed document compartments resist tampering. You should have had that information in your Preliminary Crew Three study guide."

"I skimmed that," Burke said. "I still tested high enough to be here."

Which marked Burke as exactly what Kagen had thought he was. Light crew. Barely above deadweight. Kagen decided he would pass on Burke's application and see if he could find someone better from the passenger ranks.

Annoyed, he said, "For a ship to maintain its lucrative Death Circus license in the Pact worlds, the status of every Condemned must be available to the Pact licensing body at all times. The instant the *Longview* passes a Spybee or comsat, the ship's Pact module sends a burst packet that relays our Condemned update to the Pact Core, who then distributes our list of available Condemned to all subscriber worlds. If you in any way screw up the unit's ability to identify the Condemned in the box, you screw up the system that keeps the Longview in the air."

Burke watched Kagen with puzzlement. "Wait. They're not dead?"

Kagen was pretty sure at that point Burke had done less than skim the study guide. While he sorted the paperwork correctly, making sure Burke watched him, he said, "No. Sometimes the owner decides to carry out Final Sentencing on the ship as soon as we're beyond the Pact World borders. But there's no real profit in that. And the *Longview* is the most profitable Death Circus registered."

"So we make a good living from killing people." Burke frowned. "If I hadn't managed to get passenger status on the *Longview,* I could have been one of the people in the boxes."

Kagen shrugged. "Everyone on the *Longview* has a story like that. We all have ugliness behind us. The trick is to not let that ugliness get back in front of us."

Burke raised an eyebrow.

Kagen had decided Burke was one breath above worthless, but gave him the same spiel he gave every potential member of Crew Three. "If you don't screw up on the *Longview,* you can get training all the way up to captaining your own ship. You can earn more money with us than with any other ship crew I know of. But if you want it—and I want it—you have to keep your record spotless, work hard, and study hard. And you can't make enemies. Or mistakes. It's a small crew, and almost everyone is trying to stay on it."

"Why? Because you all love the smell of burning bodies? Love taking people to their deaths?"

"We transport people who have already been categorized *Dead, Still Breathing* to places that have uses for people like that. If we didn't, someone else would, and we keep all our Condemned clean and safe and healthy until they get where they're going—which cannot be said for any other Death Circus out there. *The Longview* is different.

"When we hit some of the big buyer worlds, you start talking to crew from other Death Circuses. Most of them just shove Class B prisoners out the airlock as soon as they hit the Pact perimeter, because all Death Circuses have to buy at least 10% Class Bs, and feeding what you can't sell costs money. Class Bs are just about impossible to sell. Every other Death Circus out there buys 90% Class A Condemned and 10% Class B Condemned."

Burke said, "And Class A Condemned are the rapists, pedophiles, murderers, and... one other..."

"Thieves," Kagen told him. So Burke had at least read *something* in the study guide.

"Right." Burke considered that for an instant. "And the Class B prisoners are basically the ones who just pissed off somebody important."

Kagen nodded. "You. Me. Half the damned universe, it seems."

"And worlds *want* to buy rapists, and pedophiles, and murderers, and thieves, but don't want to buy people who didn't actually commit real crimes..."

Kagen said, "Have you ever heard of gladiators? The Shorgah Arena?"

"No."

27

"It's big on slaver worlds. Slave owners buy men other people want to see die, and they pit them against each other in a ring. They get rid of problem slaves that way, too, but there have been a couple times that policy turned around to bite them. So they like to get bad guys from much tenderer worlds. Pact worlds breed tender bad guys because they never come up against any real resistance."

"That's vile."

"It's a polite way for the Pact worlds to get rid of their worst citizens without ever having to get their own hands dirty. The slaver worlds buy women, too, of course. Women are easy to sell—the younger and prettier, the better, but slaver worlds usually have reju, so they can turn and old woman into a young woman, and keep her young and healthy and unmarked as long as they want."

"And we're a part of that. I'm not sure I want to go for Crew Three. I might just get off on the next non-Pact, non-Slaver world we come to."

"Always an option," Kagen said, shrugging. "There's more to this than you're seeing, I think—but there are also plenty of other people desperate to get the job you don't think you want."

CHAPTER FOUR

Kagen

Kagen was heading into the mess hall with the rest of Crew Three when Melie, who was Crew Two Gold, pulled him aside and waved the rest of his unit on.

"Congratulations," she said. "You passed Crew Two eligibility, and I've chosen you as Crew Two Green. You're the first person I've seen in ages who passed Crew Two eligibility the first time through."

He had just finished decontaminating the shuttles after unloading the final twenty-one units from each of them, and had showered the stink of burning humans off of his skin. And had been trying to decide whether to give Burke another chance or to tell him he'd failed and wait for another passenger to pass the eligibility exam. It had been a brutal day.

And suddenly it was better.

"Someone moving up, or someone moving out?" he asked.

"Both." She grinned. "Willett passed his Captain's

exam and got his license while we were on Cairefon, and the last Spybee we passed had a stack of offers for him. He's going to captain a TFN starcruiser for a salary that makes my eyeballs bleed. So everyone whose tests and promotion points are in order step promotes. You were short your time in grade for promotion, but you did well as Three Gold and the captain himself approved my request to move you to Two Green."

The captain himself. This was the sort of attention Kagen had been working for since the first day he worked as Three Green. If important people noticed him, and sided with him, The Dream would become real.

"Thank you," he said. "Are you staying on as Two Gold?"

"Not a chance. Mash goes Gold tonight." And then she said, "You're the first one we've had in a while who got through the exam on the first try. I'll bet you're aiming for higher."

"Captain," Kagen said. "I at least want to qualify on the captain's exam. I want to get my own ship."

"Me, too." Melie smiled. "Skip mess with Three. You'll eat next hour with Two. Right now I have just enough time to introduce you to the Sleepers."

They left mess together, and for the first time Kagen found himself facing the always-locked exit to the top-level private ship gravdrop. Melie palmed them through.

"I still find the Sleeper bays unsettling," Melie told him. "You've only seen them from the shuttle bays below. Looking up, it's all darkness and the bottoms of walkways. You won't understand how... big... this all is until you've seen it from the inside."

He'd never been through the second doors before, so she pointed out landmarks he needed.

"Crew One duty room," she said, and pointed down the corridor to the left. "Don't go in there. It's the jump room for whichever Crew One pulls third-hand standby when we're on alert. And on your right is the owner's quarters," she said and pointed to a dimly lit corridor. "If you so much as walk down that passage, you're out on the next world we hit, no matter what sort of world it is. Don't get curious, don't forget."

They reached a crossing passage with signs saying SLEEPERS LEVEL ONE, and Melie pointed to the palm-lock that opened the Sleeper bays.

"As soon as you accept the crew position, your palm code will be added to Level Two areas," she said, and pressed the palm-lock, The door slid open.

Before him lay rows of containers stacked floor to ceiling on either side of narrow corridors. They were, he realized, more complex versions of the storage units he'd been using for the last several years to bring the Condemned up from the surfaces of the worlds with which the *Longview* contracted.

"What are all the extra connectors on the containers?" he asked.

She turned and gave him a long stare and a slow head-shake. "Don't. Ask."

"You know and can't tell?"

Her voice dropped so low he had to move his ear to just centimeters from her lips to hear what she was saying. "I don't know. Nobody knows. Not even the captain. I think they're something the owner invented for sorting the Condemned, figuring out which ones will be the most valu-able where, and then marketing those people directly to the worlds that will pay the most for them. According to a name I can't mention, the *Longview's* owner is the richest Death

Circus franchisee in existence. My source says by about twenty times. And the *Longview* buys the most Condemned, but percentage-wise sells the fewest. So the ones the ship sells have to be going for unbelievable prices. *Have* to be. Because this is also the biggest and most expensive Death Circus ship in existence. And it pays crew the best."

Her lips pressed against his ear. "In here, if we're quiet, we can mention this," she told him. "If you're not in the Sleeper stacks, though, say nothing. Ever."

She pulled back. "We're gravdropping down to Level Ten. I'm just going to show you Ten Port and Starboard today. It's the smallest level, and you're new. You and I will do status sweeps on Ten together twice. Then you'll do ten on your own, and your Gold will make sure you didn't miss anything. Then you'll do Ten on the first day of the week and Nine on the third. You'll have a lot of other duties, too, but this is the most important one."

They gravdropped slowly down through the rows and stacks, and Kagen spotted green lights on some, yellow lights on a few, and red lights on many. He pointed them out.

Melie said, "Green means we have at least one bidder for that unit. We off-load those to the world that has bid the highest by the time we reach it. Yellow means the individual in the unit is new. Those will go red or green eventually. The study guides say going red means no one has bid or signaled interest... but sometimes they go red within a few hours of the Condemned's arrival, and sometimes they go green, *then* go red. And sometimes they're red for years."

"So green is usually Class A, red is usually Class B?"

"Good. I didn't have to tell you that. You did the extra levels of the exam study."

He nodded. "Figured I might not need them for Class Two, but that I'd need them for captain."

She grinned. "Actually, according to the captain, that part of the course you only need to qualify for owner. That and having just buckets of money. But I studied them, too."

"Is the owner considering selling?"

Melie shrugged. "I don't think so. And I don't know anyone who's bought a Death Circus franchise. But the captain said the owner added ownership training to each level of the testing so we'd understand what we were doing. The captain said as far as he can tell, no other Death Circus franchisee offers this."

Kagen filed that information away.

They hit Level Ten and pushed out of the gravdrop to the lowest walkway. All the way down, Kagen had been watching the rows upon rows of long containers disappearing into the darkness, and he'd been trying to count. Trying to get a sense of how many Sleepers the ship carried. He couldn't. Not even a rough guess."

"How many are there?" he asked her.

"I don't know. None of us do, and we all want to. That is another piece of information the owner keeps off the records."

"You could always count the units."

She laughed. "No. We couldn't. And if you decide you like being here, and you want to earn a captain's license without having to sell your soul and indenture your body, you'll leave this alone. It's one of the stipulations of service, which you'll get later today. You get to see this first so you'll understand the scope of your new duties. And then you have two options. Agree to the terms and accept Crew Two, or move to passenger status and get off the ship at the first world that fits your Acceptable Alternative stats."

"That seems extreme."

"Remember when I said the owner is doing something different here?"

"Yes."

"The stipulations you'll agree to regarding sharing information about this ship and what's on it are part of that. And realize that the owner is *not* playing. We veridicate after every off-ship we do, and if we don't pass veridication, we're not allowed back on the ship. We sleep in whatever Needle we end up in until some other ship will take us."

"That's harsh."

"It is. Don't count, don't dig for information you're not permitted to have, *never* get drunk or drugged and run your mouth when you're on an away team or on leave. Crew positions on the *Longview* pay five times more per level than pay on any other Death Circus ship, and officer positions pay ten times more. But that's just the start. If you do the owner's recommended investments, you can increase your pay way over that." She glanced sidelong at him. "And before you ask, you'll get the information pack with the recommended investments if you accept Crew Two placement. I've been Crew Two for my full six years now, I've done the recommended investments, but went in for more than the recommended amount, and with my Crew One raise—even assuming I wash out of captain training—I'll have enough money to buy a small in-system personal ship by the end of my Crew One minimum term. I can do better if I stay the maximum, and much, much better if I make officer."

Kagen heard the screams of the burning behind him. Before him, though, lay the clean, silent deeps of space. The possibility of his own ship within reach in twelve years, if he could make the grade, get the promotions, and keep his crew record clean.

Freedom, space, a way to get away from the regulated worlds and move out from under the ever-watching eye of the Pact, and away from slaver worlds, and maybe set up on an indie world as a transport. Or a privateer.

The Dream, and everything it took him away from, was sliding into reach.

———

"This is your quarters," Melie told him. "As the Crew Green, you get 3-B. You've been Crew Green before."

Kagen nodded. "For two months. But I remember the drill. First out of bed, scrub the head before anyone else is awake, respond to all alarms, make sure the crew unit is secure; if there's an emergency, make sure everyone in the unit is in shipsuits. I am Green, I am expendable."

Melie said, "You and me both. When you're crew, you never get to forget what it means to be Green."

"You're doing Green duty in Crew One?"

"That's not the half of it. You're probably going to be Green for six months, until one of your current Blues decides not to stick it out for the next promotion. At which point you'll bump up and the new Three Gold will jump at the chance to be Two Green. But me? I'm looking at up to three years as One Green, because Joze is only two years in as Two Gold. And there are only two of us. With three years left on his eligibility, he's not going to leave until he makes first mate or runs out his clock. And I don't move up until he makes officer or leaves."

"And we have a brand new first mate who has five years to promote to captain, and a relatively new captain."

Melie nodded.

"But you're Crew One."

She grinned. "That I am. And you know I'm sticking. I want to make captain here. But either way, I'll qualify as captain and do the licensing, and if I run out my clock, I'll buy my own ship. And I *could* be the one who's in the right place at the right time to be captain here."

"So you did the full Crew Two run," he said.

She nodded.

"Any advice?"

"Probably not any that you need. Most of the crew in Two is not pushing for captain. Most of them haven't done the investments. They love spending time in rec, and spending their downtime on the fun worlds having fun. So you study like a beast for the exams, and you take them every single time you're eligible. Aim to step-promote every year—if you go faster, you won't have as much money saved up. Do all the owner-recommended investments, live cheap, and at bare minimum you'll get out of here with enough money to make a good down payment on your ship. What you do from there is up to you."

"And best case..."

"Best case, you become my first mate, and when I move on to my own ship, you become *Longview's* captain."

Other members of Crew Two started coming in. They would wash before their meal, then go up to the Mess Hall to eat together.

Kagen knew the people in Two, but only as an underling. As Green, he was still an underling, but now he was *their* underling.

Mash was the new Two Gold, Taryn was the new Two Silver, and Lindar, Porth, and Aya were all Blues. Each of them touched fingertips with him as they came in, and each said, "Welcome to Two, greenie." Each then touched finger-tips with Melie and said, "Do well in One."

It was the way all crew got welcomed into a new unit, and the way all promoted crew left. It always seemed casual, but it wasn't. The words were precisely the same, and they hid the motivations, prejudices, and passions of those who said them.

Incoming crew frequently knew—or at least knew about —their seniors. Existing unit crew knew about the reputations of incoming juniors. But living with them in the close quarters of the unit, eating with them at every meal of every day, spending recreational or study time with them, they would be forced into a closeness that Kagen found difficult to manage.

He had dealt with the issue by burying himself in study, working for promotion points, and taking every grade exam the instant he became eligible. It let him avoid people as much as possible, and the distance he kept had made it easier for him to keep the distance necessary to be effective in Gold. He'd never had friends he had to discipline, because he didn't have friends. No one ever accused him of favoritism, because he didn't have favorites.

He hoped that same would work to his advantage in Two.

Mash, as the new Gold, said, "Present your connector."

Kagen reached out with his right hand. The pale circle of luminescent ink—something exclusively used by the crew of the *Longview*—marked the location of embedded data-transfer nanoclusters that allowed the instant exchange of information.

"Your Level Two Green Packet and Orders," Mash said, and the two clasped right hands. Their connectors linked up, and Kagen instantly had full access to his orders, his room assignment, the crew-level promotion sheets of the people in his unit, and his schedule.

"I'm missing my list of recommended investments," he said.

Mash's face darkened, and his gaze flicked from Melie back to Kagen. "You'll get them when you need them, greenie."

Mash, he realized, was a man who needed to be the biggest bull in the room.

Kagen didn't miss the expressions on either Melie's or Mash's face as they stared each other down.

"So. You're sticking me with your... *protégé?*" Mash asked, and his emphasis on the word suggested a relationship considerably less professional than mentor and student.

Melie stared right back. "Are you already failing at your job requirements as Two Gold?"

She outranked him. She clearly didn't like him. He clearly didn't like her—this was information that had never filtered down to Crew Three.

If Melie had time to force the issue with Mash, his dislike for her would get itself transferred to Kagen with the same speed that his Green packet had arrived.

And Melie wasn't going to be around to help him deal with Mash. She was going to be in her own unit, busy dealing with her own stint as Green.

The Dream flickered before his eyes. Mash could ruin him—Kagen had never sabotaged anyone in Three, because he didn't like or dislike his underlings. But he knew how sabotage could be accomplished easily within any portion of the three years Mash could remain as Crew Two Gold.

Kagen had to side with his crew leader, no matter how much he didn't want to.

"Not a problem," he told Mash. "I wasn't planning on wasting my money gambling on something speculative anyway. I just wanted to see what was on the sheet."

He saw the look of shock on Melie's face, the look of satisfaction on Mash's.

And in the moment he said it, he realized that he had no other way to get the recommended investments if Mash didn't pass them to him. Packets were coded. No crew member could share his or accidentally pass it to someone else.

Mash would hold Kagen to his word... he'd said that he wasn't interested. Mash—biggest bull in the room—would remind Kagen of his words if ever he tried to recant. So Kagen would lose up to three prime years of building his capital to buy his ship that he could not get back, and the early years were the most important. Compound interest made early investments vastly more profitable than investments made late.

And just as bad, if the look on Melie's face was any indication, he had just murdered all hope of her recommending him again as the two of them moved up the promotion ladder. He'd just spit on her for championing him in front of a man who was not just her subordinate, but her enemy.

Third, he'd put himself on the wrong side of the career fence, marked himself to those others in his unit who were on the promotion track as light crew who didn't understand the value of *this* ship, *this* job, *this* opportunity.

Worst of all, he knew why he'd done it. The pathetic voice of We that still wailed inside of him, that still bent before trouble rather than standing against it, had cried out that he was about to be destroyed.

And he had listened.

He'd betrayed his ally, had sided with his enemy, had claimed We over I.

He would have done anything to have that moment back. But the moment was gone, the damage done.

He'd made an unrecoverable mistake.

A man who could not hold onto his principles against the threat of disapproval was not a man who would ever be captain. Not of this ship.

Not of any ship.

CHAPTER FIVE

Kagen

Alone, Kagen worked his way through the stacks on Level Ten. The place made his skin crawl. It wasn't as bad when Melie had done the first two rounds with him, though those rounds hadn't been pleasant.

She'd spoken to him only when she absolutely had to as she showed him the process of keeping each Condemned core connected into the system and fully charged.

She made sure he understood that any disconnect or unit failure would mean his job—that every active core unit was valuable to the owner and the crew responsible for the few units that had ever failed had been dropped off at the Needle of whatever world was next on the circuit and left to fend for themselves.

Core integrity was the number one priority of every member of Two. *Everything* else came second.

But while she did her job well, that was all she did. She didn't hear him if he offered a personal remark or tried to apologize. She gave him the two days of training he needed, and then she was gone to her own duties as Crew Two Green.

And he was left with Mash, who went through after he had made his rounds and claimed to have found errors Kagen had made, even though Kagen knew he had not made them. Three weeks into his stint as Two Green, Mash still treated him like a complete waste of skin.

Kagen worked his way alone through the dimly lit stacks, feeling the ghosts of his past and the ghosts of his future crowding in on him, and he tried to focus on the work he was doing.

The still bodies in the stacks made it hard for him to maintain his romantic notion of the owner as some escaped Class B prisoner made good and determined to save his fellow Class B prisoners. The endless rows of the officially dead stored in cold, hard storage units spoke of some horrific purpose that he could not begin to comprehend. He did his best not to look at their faces through the transparent inspection covers. The people inside did not breathe. They did not move.

They were not dead, but they were the same as dead. They had been reported dead back on their home worlds, with the terms of their executions fulfilled.

Officially dead, but not entirely dead—stored, with large amounts of energy expended in storing them.

All of the cores—the storage units with their locking seals stamped Death Sentence Carried Out and their heavy-duty power cables and complex end-caps that performed functions no one could guess at—were full in Level Ten. All of them were red-lighted. All of them would always be red-lighted. Level Ten was designated permanent storage.

Each person in each core had been passed over for

purchase, had been categorized as unsaleable, and had been sentenced to eternity within the chamber that held him. Or her.

Men and women, young and old, lay motionless, eyes closed, lungs forever stilled, captive forever, with enormous amounts of power running through their units, not alive but not dead either.

Kagen's imagination ran wild. To store the not-entirely-dead in such a fashion, the owner had to be doing something with them. Had he discovered a way to use them as filters to process vast quantities of designer nanoviruses? Had he discovered that souls were real, and found a way to sell theirs? No one would spend the vast fortune it had taken to store the bodies of countless nearly dead for as close to eternity as technology could reach unless there was some tremendous payoff for him. It was entirely too cheap and easy to simply kill people and dump their bodies into space.

So why did this place with its red lights exist?

He rounded the corner in the narrow aisle, asking himself that question, and this one time, his head was up and he was looking directly at the ident screen on the core directly in front of him as he came around the corner.

It said We-T74G.

He froze.

He stared at the screen, frowning, trying to look at the letters and numbers and see a different combination, to make it clear to himself that his mind was playing tricks on him.

But below the identity designator, he read, "Origin: The People's Home of Truth and Fairness 14-B."

The date was right around the time he'd been exiled to the Needle, sentenced to work alone until he was ready to starve to death or throw himself into space to rejoin the We.

She might have come aboard in a transport unit the same day he'd been taken in as a passenger by the *Longview*. He had worked his way past her and checked her unit half a dozen times without seeing her.

But this time, he found himself frozen, staring at a face he could not believe he was seeing. She was the girl of his memory—unchanged—though he could no longer see the little grin she'd aimed at him when the two of them were doing Weeding Duty, separated by the wire mesh that kept We First apart from We Second.

Her dark hair curled up around her face as if gravity meant nothing to it, as it had always done.

Her lips were full and perfect. Her brow arched. Her jaw was smooth and firm. She would never have been sentenced with the crime of Property of Beauty.

She was the girl he'd kissed and called "Love" during the morning recitation of the *Truth of We*.

She'd been Condemned when he'd been exiled.

He had never before considered that she might be sentenced to death for what he had done. But she would have been. There was no justice on a People's Home of Truth and Fairness.

Her crime would have been Property of Love. He looked lower on the ident screen.

"Murder Grand, four counts."

That was impossible. They'd lied about her to make an example of her. To make sure she would never kiss another boy—and to make sure, as well, that anyone who saw what happened to her wouldn't either.

So they'd sentenced her for murder, which meant she could not be offered Return to Citizenship in the lake of fire.

Then they'd sent her away so some rich ship owner could flip a switch and turn her off forever.

On another world, the two of them could have been together. On some sane Pact world, they could have been friends. Could have been lovers. Could have been together their whole lives.

He rested his fingertips on her core. He whispered, "If you had known it would end like this, would you still have done it? Would you still have kissed me back? Locked away in a storage unit in the bottom of a spaceship for the rest of forever, never knowing what you were being used for, what precious commodity was being drained from your body and sold..."

Her still, frozen face haunted him. "No," she seemed to say. "Of course I wouldn't have kissed you. Look what they did to me because I did."

He looked at the future that lay before him. He had sold his future among the stars because he'd been unwilling to stand firm against Mash—just as he had sold the girl whose smile he had loved to Death for the price of a kiss.

He had failed, and failed again. His dreams were dead. His future was ruined

Only one path remained to him.

Melie

When the emergency panel went off on Level Ten, Melie was asleep.

But she was Green, so she dragged herself upright, threw on her shipsuit, and gravdropped to Ten with the suit accelerating her passage.

The units on Ten were usually stable. She'd seen Mash's reports about Two Green making mistakes, but as

Level One crew, she had access to the process flows from Level Ten, and Kagen hadn't made any mistakes.

Someone had come along after him, had tampered with what he'd done, had played with the public time-set to make it look like the mistake had been made when the unit was checked, and had then signed himself into the unit as himself and had corrected the error and sent notification to the captain.

She suspected this time Mash had set one unit low enough to drop to alarm status before Kagen did his next rounds—which would put Kagen before the captain, the first mate, and the owner's representative, unless the owner himself decided to weigh in.

She hit Ten fast and followed the overhead running lights and the directional signal on her wristcom through the stacks.

And there she found Kagen. With him stood a girl who was touching his face with a mixture of joy and dismay—and beside the two of them was the shattered Sentence Seal that had once secured the core unit of We-T74G.

"I do remember you," the girl was saying, running her fingers across Kagen's cheeks and lips and jaw.

"Oh, hell," Melie whispered.

Kagen turned to stare at her. He stepped in front of the girl. "Before you say anything, I'm taking her place in the box. She did nothing to deserve a death sentence, and I'm the reason she was sentenced. If I can't be the captain of my own ship, if I can't fix what I've done wrong here, I can at least fix what I did to her. Just help me get into the core, lock it back, figure out a way to reseal it..."

And the girl looked from Kagen to Melie and said, "He didn't know, and he doesn't understand. But I have to go back in. As much as I want to be with him, I can't stay here."

Melie said, "Kagen, you idiot. You screwed up every-thing. You— We... whatever your number is. I'll help you into the box. Maybe we can still fix all of this."

The girl said, "Just call me Lithra."

And then, behind Melie, the owner's representative, Shay, said, "Unfortunately, We-T74G's unit has already reported re-activation."

Melie cringed and turned to face her.

Shay continued, "No one can go into that core now. We're going to have to file an incident report with the Death Circus administration about one of our official executions appearing to return to life... and all three of you are going to have to stand before the captain and the first mate. You will probably have to face the owner, too, instead of me. He was furious when the alarm went off in his quarters."

The security detail came around the corner, and snapped restraints on Kagen and Melie. Lithra walked between them, unrestrained but cooperative.

CHAPTER SIX

Kagen

The captain sat at the big chair in his private mess. On his right sat the first mate. The chair to his left was empty. When everyone came through the door, he looked past Melie, Lithra, Kagen, and the security detail to the owner's representative. "He says he's too angry to deal with them rationally. You're in the third seat, Shay."

Kagen had never seen the owner's representative before. She was stunning. Long, straight red hair, impossibly green eyes, incredible body. He wondered what her story was—how she'd ended up among the *Longview's* misfits.

Shay sighed heavily. "I don't know why he does this. He's never happy with what I decide."

Then she took her seat and said, "I have the comlink open to the owner's quarters. He may or may not comment, but he'll get the full recording. So go ahead when you're ready."

The captain nodded. "He have a preference in which one we interview first?"

Shay murmured into her shipcom and came back with, "Lithra. He wants to know why the idiot took her out of the box."

The captain muttered, "I'd ask the *idiot* that question," but Lithra had already stepped forward.

"When I was We-T74G on The People's Home of Truth and Fairness 14-B, the man behind me was a boy. And he was my only friend, even though we never dared speak to each other. You know how the PHTF worlds are. And one day he kissed me, and did it in front of Speakers for We. He was exiled to the Needle, where he was to stay until he died, while I was sentenced as a criminal of Property: Love, and handed to the Speakers to be their plaything.

"I did not want to have them touch me," she said. "I decided I would rather die—so I attacked the first man who came into the cell where I was held, and was lucky enough to kill him. I took the weapon I found on his body, and used it to kill the next three men who entered the cell. One of the men was the Head Speaker, and the fact that he was dead and that I had killed him made it mandatory that I be sentenced as a Class A prisoner. And because I was a Class A prisoner, I was untouched until I was sent to the Death Circus.

"If he had not kissed me, I would never have survived to escape PHTF 14-B. Even if the Speakers had not taken me before I became an official citizen to be one of their toys, to be abused and killed as so many other women were, I would have spent the rest of my life in one of the breeding factories. If unending cycles of pregnancy and childbirth didn't kill me, volunteering for the Room of Release or Return to

Citizenship when I could no longer bear children would have.

"I request that you absolve him for the actions he took tonight, even though there will be problems that arise from them. He acted out of love and great courage—he was willing to go into my box and take my death sentence to give me my freedom."

"We cannot let him go unpunished. He destroyed the owner's property, acted against the rules he had agreed to obey, and has put the charter of the *Longview* at risk," the captain said. "He cannot remain in his current position as crew."

"I agree," the first mate said.

The girl looked from captain to first mate, clearly frightened. "I do not understand."

The owner's representative said, "He will be sentenced based on his actions. He must be. Otherwise, there can be no justice." She gave the girl a long look, and eventually the girl nodded. "You faced the same justice he faces. Think on that. And now it is time for you to return to your core. It's been repaired."

"No!" Kagen shouted. "You can't condemn her to nothingness again! She did nothing wrong!"

"We must," Shay said. "This ship cannot maintain its charter if we do not."

Lithra turned to the crew who were on security duty, and said, "I'll go with you, and I won't cause you any problems." And then she turned to the captain. "May I thank him before I go?"

The captain said, "Yes. I suppose."

Lithra came to Kagen, and reached up on her toes and kissed him once, passionately. "Thank you for trying to save me. I have always loved you. And I always will."

She wrapped her arms around him and held him tightly, pressing her head to his chest. "I will remember the sound of your heart beating. Always."

He pulled against the ungiving restraints around his wrists, desperate to hold her close to him. He could do nothing. With his eyes filling with tears, he whispered, "You were my only love. You are. You'll always be." He swallowed hard, and she pulled away from him and walked between the crew members who took her back to her core. Back to nothing, forever.

"Melie," the captain said, "I'll hear from you next unless there are any objections."

Both the owner's representative and the first mate shook their heads, indicating they had no objections.

So the captain said, "Do you have any idea what caused this behavior by your choice for Two Green?"

Melie winced on hearing Kagen described in that fashion. Kagen didn't blame her. He'd certainly not turned out to be the man she'd chosen to move up to Two.

She said, "I've been investigating Mash for the last three months for intimidation of other crew members, and for attempting to fill all crew positions with his people. I admit that I somewhat misused Three Gold Kagen when I brought him into Two as my choice for Green. I'd previously made sure to mention Kagen among my Two unit as my best guess for eventual captain of the *Longview,* and while this was in fact true, I made sure to state it more than once in front of Mash."

Kagen watched her looking from face to face across the table. He could see her trying to figure out how all three listeners were taking this information. "So Mash was already inclined to hate Kagen. When Mash step-promoted into Two-Gold the same day Kagen became Two Green,

Mash saw Kagen as a better-qualified rival for the job he planned to get, and further, as someone he needed to take down."

She sighed. "I could not warn Kagen about what I was doing without damaging the credibility of my investigation. I have not been able to explain my treatment of him to him —and I have not been kind.

"So he'll have to confirm this for you, but I suspect he took his treatment by Mash and me as signs that he had made an unfixable mistake, and I further suspect he thought he had lost his future on the *Longview*.

"You see, Mash has been going behind him, sabotaging his work on Level Ten while ostensibly checking after him. He's been writing Kagen up for every mistake he claims to have found. I was waiting for that noxious..." She stopped herself from saying whatever she had been planning to say, and started over. "I was waiting for Two Gold to submit his formal *Request for Dismissal of Crew* on Kagen before I sent my own results to you. I wanted you to be able to independently compare Mash's documentation of errors with mine."

She pulled her shoulders back and lifted her chin. "One of my associates from Two says Mash has just about completed his dismissal request form. My informant expects it to go to you..." her gaze flicked to the clock, and she sighed, "...in six or seven more hours. Once Mash submits that request, I can bring forward everything I've found out about what he's been doing. This will include falsifying records on three other talented subordinate crew members, which resulted in one crewman being removed from crew and left without recommendation in the nearest Needle on our circuit, and the other two leaving the *Longview* before he could create his reports on them. I cannot prove the cases on the two who quit, but if you can search Mash's private files before he can delete them, you will probably find falsified documentation."

Kagen tried not to look as stunned as he felt.

Melie had been working to get rid of Mash.

She'd still thought he would have qualified as captain eventually.

He was truly an idiot.

"And your attempt to get the girl he'd liberated from her core back into her box before anyone found out?" Shay asked Melie.

Melie dropped her head. "I was hoping to save both his career and my investigation."

"Because...?" the owner's representative prodded.

"Because I thought both of these actions would be in the best interests of the owner, the crew, Kagen's career, and my own career."

"Both the owner and I are inclined to agree that they were," Shay said, and glanced over at the captain. "The owner wants your first thoughts."

"If that damned report were in my hands already, I could simply demote her back to Two Gold and let her serve there for an extra year without counting that as overage on her time in grade."

"I'll be happy to get the report in your hands within the next five minutes," the first mate said. "I'll simply go to Mash, let him know it looks like One Green may be opening up, and ask him if he has anything he can present to suggest himself as a suitable candidate for the opening."

"Do it," the captain said, and the first mate shot out of the room like a man on fire.

He was as good as his word.

He wasn't even back when the captain's wristcom whispered to him, and he nodded.

He turned to Melie. "That's his report. Can you bring up yours?"

She nodded. "If you can remove my restraints, I can transfer it to you from here."

He nodded to the crew member standing guard behind Melie. "Take them off her."

Kagen watched the crew member tap her wristcom and an instant later, the captain's wristcom whispered to him again.

He flicked a finger, and both reports appeared in the space in front of him, reversed from Kagen's perspective. He flipped through each at tremendous speed, and after just moments, he said, "All right. The security detail is going to be delayed here just a bit longer. When I've finished with you and Kagen, I want night security and day security to go together, armored and armed, and pick up Mash and move him to the brig. I'll come with you to get him out of his room without giving him the chance to destroy his private files, and to present the charges once you have restrained him.

"Melie, you have two choices. You can either take what you've earned and cash out now, or you can be demoted to Two Gold with no promotion for one year, but no disqualification for the time spent."

She looked a little pale, but she said, "I'll stay."

And then the captain turned to Kagen.

"Do you have anything to say for yourself?"

Kagen considered. "I did what seemed to me the most just and proper thing I could, based on the situation I believed myself to be in and on what I knew of the girl in the core unit." He paused, still thinking, then decided to add, "Because of who Lithra is to me, and because she should never have been sentenced to death, I would do the same thing again if opportunity presented itself."

The captain sighed. "Thank you for your honesty, no matter how damaging to your case it happens to be."

He stared down at the table, drumming the fingers of his right hand on the surface in an irritable, quick pattern.

He sighed again. "You have done a brilliant, irreversible job of destroying what has been one of the most promising careers I've seen anyone put together. You have demonstrated an impulsiveness that makes you impossible to keep on as a crew member. You have destroyed the shipowner's property, have released a convicted criminal from a mandatory death sentence, and have allowed emotion to sway you into dereliction of duty.

"By any standard of space law, I have the absolute right to drop you off at the nearest Needle with no papers, no recommendation, and no money, and let you fend for yourself. Furthermore, that is the sentence that best fits within my guidelines as *Longview* captain."

Kagen braced himself.

The captain looked at the ship's representative. "Does the owner wish to involve himself in sentencing?"

Kagen watched Shay listen to her shipcom, nod, murmur something he could not hear, and then say, "As you wish."

She turned to the Kagen directly. "The owner wishes to pass sentence himself, if the captain will defer." She turned to the captain.

"I'll defer. Happily, in this instance."

"Very well. Kagen, you have been given two choices. Because the owner was moved by Lithra's story of her love for you, and by what you tried to do for her—ignoring the criminality of what you did—he has chosen to impose a lighter sentence than what the captain would have to make.

"Your first choice is to select a world on our circuit on which you'll debark. You'll take with you all money you earned on the *Longview,* and will leave with only your record up to the end of your stint in Three Gold. No mention will be made of your promotion, your test scores or points toward promotion. You will go out as a Three Gold who chose to terminate with the *Longview* in search of other employment, and who became a passenger when you made this decision so that we could train your replacement while you were aboard."

He looked at her and swallowed hard.

"You wish to say something?"

"That's... very generous."

"Yes," she agreed. "It is." She stared into his eyes, and he felt himself wanting to squirm.

"Your other option is... very different. The owner has offered to make a core unit available to you. If you choose to take this option you will wait, exactly as Lithra is waiting. At some point in the future, the laws under which she has been sentenced to death may be changed, or the government that sentenced her may cease to exist in its current political structure, or the Pact may change its ruling on the death sentence, at which point her sentence will be negated, and she will be freed. If this happens, you will be freed along with her. Neither of you will be any older than you are now, and you will at that time be able to pursue whatever relationship you may desire."

She was still looking into his eyes, searching for some truth about him that he could not begin to guess.

"Understand," she continued, "that there is no guarantee she will ever be released, and hence, no guarantee that you will ever be released. There is no guarantee that you will still love each other if you are, and no guarantee if you do that you will have any sort of future together. Your current existence will stop when you are in the core, and may never resume. Your money will accrue for you—the owner will treat it as a Level Two crew investment, since this appears to have been the point of contention that caused your dispute with Mash. But there is no guarantee that you will ever claim it."

He stood there, feeling Lithra's arms around him, feeling her lips pressed to his once more. She was still alive —if only after a fashion—and she had known him, had loved him.

He could make it in the universe with what the owner had generously offered to him. He could find another ship, become part of another crew, and someday he might once again have the chance to own a ship and captain it through the stars.

But he was on a ship in which the woman he loved loved him back. She was locked away in one of those cores... and she had not been afraid to re-enter it. She had almost seemed eager to go back. He had earlier been willing to go into the core without any hope of ever seeing her again.

How could he turn down the chance to go in with the hope that one day the two of them might be together?

"I'll take the core," he said.

The owner's representative nodded. "I thought you might."

CHAPTER SEVEN

This Criminal

There was death. And now there isn't.

This criminal wakes—but the waking is all wrong. Sunlight blinds its eyes, and it cries from fear and shock, and arms hold it, and a voice comforts it.

This criminal has a body it cannot control. It cannot speak. It cannot ask.

It remembers what it was, but that is no longer what it is.

Yet the voice comforts it. The arms hold it.

After a while, this criminal stops fighting.

And it sleeps.

AFTERWORD

This series wasn't born in the usual manner. Most of the time, if I come up with a series idea, it's because I sat down and intentionally brainstormed concepts until I figured one out.

But I would have sworn the only stories I was going to write in Settled Space would have Cadence Drake as the main character.

Here's how I tripped over *The Longview.*

I was writing *Warpaint,* the sequel to *Hunting the Corrigan's Blood.* And I was having an awful time getting the scale of the ship in my head. I'd done a ship layout on quad paper, and had my scale figured out. I knew where things were. But the drawing was about seven inches long from nose to tail, and Cady's ship was about 280 feet (about 87 meters) from nose to tail.

I was having trouble looking at that tiny line drawing and visualizing Cady and her crew moving around inside the ship, and, as frequently happens when I'm struggling with a story problem, I had this crazy idea.

I thought, *I can just build the damn thing in Minecraft,*

and go inside it and walk around and then I'll know what it's like in there.

So I figured one block for one meter and I carefully laid out the ship, following my schematic. Built the whole thing, furnished it, filled it with secret areas and notes to myself about who went where (stuck on signs.)

And then, because it was so incredibly useful to stand in the middle of the ship and know exactly what my characters could see and do, where they could go, and how they could get there, I built the other two ships from the *Cadence Drake* series so far.

And then I built the *Bailey's Irish Space Station* for the upcoming third novel in the series, *The Wishbone Conspiracy.*

I was hooked, you see. Having these places that I could walk around in was fun...but better than being fun, the places I'd built were talking to me. They were telling me stories.

But then I ran out of things to build.

The little voice in my head whispered, *How about building an ancient, mysterious spaceship from the days before TFN travel, when people were trying to colonize space in giant sleeper ships? Just for fun. No pressure. You aren't going to use it. You'll just build it.*

I may have an odd idea of fun, but I started building that mammoth ship. And floating through its vast reaches, feeling the dark and the weight around it, I realized its first inhabitants never reached their destination. I understood that when it was salvaged, the person who bought it and retrofitted it was going to have to be someone odd. Someone with a secret plan, and a hidden past.

Someone with a use for a ship that big that had absolutely nothing to do with the ship's apparent purpose.

Suddenly I wasn't building a spaceship for fun anymore. I had to know what was going on.

And here we are. I hope you'll accompany me through the next episode, when we'll rejoin the crew of *The Longview* as they deal with the extraordinary interstellar ruckus caused by *The Selling of Suzee Delight*... and look a little deeper into the lives of the folks from this tale.

Holly Lisle
  Thursday, April 3, 2014

THE SELLING OF SUZEE DELIGHT

EXCERPT

Tales from the Longview: Episode 2 — The
Selling of Suzee Delight

CHAPTER 1

Suzee Delight — Preliminary Death Sentencing Interview #1

Danyal Travers, SPORC Capital Offenses Interviewer, Cheegoth:

Prisoner, you have stated your professional name and ident. For the record, who are you?

Suzee Delight, First Courtesan, Court of the Diamond Dome, Mariposa Pleasure City, Cheegoth:

What I am was chosen for me when I was nine years old, when the Educational Selectors discovered that I could sing and dance and play musical instruments and draw pretty pictures—and when they also discovered that my aptitude for science and mathematics was even stronger than my aptitude for the arts. Wishing to suppress my math-

ematical and science interests and to encourage my entertainment abilities, my Selector removed me from the
General Consumer cohort, named me Tawny Girl, and
placed me on the Introductory Arts and Pleasures track. I
was trained to be a consort.

Because I exhibited superior skills and ability to learn
and equally because I was obedient, when I was twelve I
was placed into Advanced Arts and Pleasures and renamed
Sweet Silver. Along with my physical and entertainment
training, I began learning languages, courtesies, and what
the Pleasure Masters refer to as Polite Observational Skills.

Danyal (interrupting): Spying.

Suzee Delight: I've heard it called that. I do not think
that is the correct word. My training teaches that as a
consort and courtesan, my service to my profession must
consist of equal parts information gathering and recording
on my clients, and the providing of entertainment and pleasure for my clients.

Third voice: Suppress that, Travers. That does not go
into the public record.

Danyal: I've deleted that. Prisoner, please continue.

Suzee Delight: By the age of seventeen, I had
learned so far beyond the rest of my Pleasure cohort that I
was moved into Masters training in Arts and Pleasures. At
that time, I was renamed Suzee Delight, and for the past six
years I have been the First Courtesan of Diamond Dome. I
have served at the direction of the Pleasure Masters, and at
the pleasure of my clients.

Danyal: While the information you have given is true,
it does not answer my question. *Who are you?*

Suzee Delight: I'm sorry. I don't understand your
question.

Danyal: You murdered the Administrators of the five most populous and powerful Pact Worlds. You did so during a seduction dance performed for all five men at once, using a knife that you could not possibly have had, hidden beneath your costume and... on... on...

(*The sound of the interviewer taking a deep breath is followed by a long silence.*)

(*Audio resumes.*)

You killed all five of them before any one could warn the others. Our holos show that you never hesitated, that you never missed a step, that not one of the men had any inkling of his danger or made any move to protect himself when you killed him.

Suzee Delight: Yes. I am a remarkable dancer. And I killed them quickly because I wished to be merciful. I had always considered them dear friends.

Danyal: Prisoner, I want an answer to the question I asked you. Someone planted you in the Diamond Dome, someone gave you the order to kill the Administrators, someone gave you the knife, someone put you up to this. Who are you really?

Suzee Delight: You are mistaken in several ways. First, I am not a *who*. I am a *what*. I am the product of my training. Every moment of my life since I was tested at the age of nine has been recorded; every action I have taken with every man and woman who has paid for pleasure from me is available to you in full holographic detail. Second, in every encounter with every client, I have acted on my training, and I have done exactly what that training has dictated I do—including the encounter for which I am now here.

Danyal: You're saying that you acted on your own—

that you murdered the five Pact Worlds Administrators—because your whore training required that you do so?

Suzee Delight: I am a courtesan. I don't know what training whores receive. My lifetime of training as a courtesan required that once I learned and verified the truth about my old friends and longtime clients—Radiva Kels, Stannal Bregat, Nethamatnu Ha, Soth Smithe, and Kiero Chenzwa—I had to stop them before they could commit the crime they planned.

And the only way I could stop them, because of the enormity of the crime they were planning and how close they were to committing it, was to kill them. They were going to legalize sla—

Third voice: OH, GOD! Delete, delete, delete! Stop the interview, get her out back to her cell, and delete that entire last bit.

(*The sound of someone pushing buttons while warnings sounded, and then a long pause.*)

Danyal: Prisoner, we'll resume this interview at a later time.

SUZEE DELIGHT

I lied to Danyal Travers. I know exactly who and what I am.

A courtesan is a whore with a good education, and what I am is the best-educated whore in the Pact Worlds—and the most famous one. I'm Suzee Delight, and from my original songs and dances and my *Paint Beautiful Pictures as Suzee Delight* Senso series, on through my instructional pleasure moves and positions, and right up to to my studio-recorded personal full-Senso sessions with famous clients, my mass-appeal products sell to more than three billion men and women across Settled Space. The Pleasure Masters make a great deal of money off of me.

As for who I am...?

Well, I'm the woman who, as a little girl, wanted to be a scientist and design custom nanoviral augmentations for GenDaring on Bailey's Irish Space Station.

When, during my Wish Conference back when I was nine, I told my Educational Selector that I wanted to leave the Pact Worlds and become a citizen of Bailey's Irish so I could make tiger people and pony people, he should have let me go.

Now—because he didn't—I'm going to destroy the whole poisonous, corrupt Pact Covenants system and every power player in it.

The five great men who had entrusted me with their pleasure and privacy had come to the Diamond Dome to make use of me... but also to write law—to modify the final language of the Covenants of the Pact.

They had a clever plan to become even richer and more powerful, though at the expense of the people they supposedly served.

And that's where I come in. The life I wanted to live was taken away from me when I was nine.

In truth, it was taken away from me when I was born, but I did not find out that I was an Assisted child and that my government would choose my life path for me until my ninth birthday.

My life—the life I wanted—was over a long time ago. My execution—if that is where I end—will be the conclusion of my long humiliation and pain.

But if I die, I'm going to bury the people who did this to me right along with me.

How?

It starts with my comment during my interview about me being nothing beyond the thing their training created.

I put that into the interview with Danyal Travers because I knew the new Administrator of Cheegoth was listening in, as were my Pleasure Masters, the Educational Selectors, and everyone else in the whole corrupt Personal Skills and Educational Tracking and Optimization system.

By stating categorically that my training required me to kill my clients once I knew and had validated that they were planning to commit a crime against the Pacts of the Covenant, I sent everyone responsible for my education back through every bit of it from the day I was old enough to toddle into General Consumer training at the age of two.

While they task ever more resources into dissecting those stored holos and figuring out where I came up with my justification for murder—and at the same time put more resources into searching for outsiders who might have somehow implanted in me a trigger they could use from afar —I have both the time and the means to contact an old client who promised to help me out should I ever find myself in a situation where I had to do something that was both right... and criminal.

CHARLIE

Charlie, the *Longview's* Mandatory Pact Covenant Observer, sat in Passenger Room 5, her Longview quarters, and on split screens watched what was being billed as the holocast of the century, presented by ever-smiling Danyal Travers, who had been covering the story for days. Each of Charlie's two screens showed a different datastream of the same event.

On the left screen, she had the official Pact Worlds coverage of the public confession and sentencing of Suzee Delight, First Courtesan of the Diamond Dome, superstar goddess of a thousand Sensos—some actually suitable for general audiences—and reputed simultaneous murderer of the Administrators of the five most important Pact Worlds.

On the right screen, she had the raw, siphoned, underground version of the same feed. If Charlie's Pact Worlds controller ever discovered that she watched unofficial feeds of anything streamed from the Pact Worlds, he would recall her and drop her citizenship level to F-10: Permanently Unemployable, Sentenced to Minimal Survival Assistance Only.

However, as long as she was assigned to the *Longview* and had Passenger Room 5 to herself, she was safe. If she did her job and made sure the Pact Worlds received a steady stream of money in exchange for their sentenced criminals, she could hope to remain aboard the *Longview,* where she was treated better than she'd ever been treated in her life, for at least a couple more years before she received mandatory rotation orders.

Charlie's only objective where her controller was concerned was to remain unremarkable—to do an average job, turn in average numbers, and in all ways be an invisible cog in the Pact Worlds' massive machine.

So she was content that the *Longview,* rumored to be the most profitable Death Circus franchise in Settled Space for its owner, only managed to stay in the middle of the pack where its profits on criminals bought and sold was concerned. How its owner made his *other* money was officially none of her concern.

Unofficially...

...Well, anything she knew, she might be able to use to her own benefit. And she'd made it her business to know a lot.

Until she found a way to use what she knew, Charlie had decided that if she received rotation or recall orders, she planned to defect. Her defection details were fuzzy, but she was getting them together.

Meanwhile, however, she was in a position to make a difference for people the Pact Worlds considered fodder.

So she watched, tense, anxious, and at the same time hopeful.

Left-side Suzee said, "I am ashamed of my actions. I betrayed the trust of five men I loved, and used my position of trust to murder them because I envied them their power."

Right-side Suzee said, "I am not ashamed of my actions. These five men betrayed the people they served. They planned to use their positions of trust and power to destroy the autonomy of the citizens they claim to represent."

The cutwork on the official version had been skillfully done. Charlie couldn't see or hear the blending between the segments that were actually Suzee's words, and those that had been inserted.

Most of Settled Space would see the raw version, would know the venom in Travers' voice as he asked her the questions, would see his eyes glitter as he envisioned her eventual fate.

Most citizens of the Pact Worlds, however, would only have access to the official version, which had little truth in it.

Left-side Suzee said, "I failed my government, my educators, my selectors, my trainers, my clients, and my profession as a courtesan—the highest calling to which any woman can aspire."

Right-side Suzee said, "I accuse my government, my educators, my selectors, my trainers, and my clients for creating laws that make being a courtesan the highest work to which any woman can aspire."

"Damned right," Charlie muttered. "You tell 'em, Suzee."

Charlie had been lucky enough to be born homely and lacking in any discernible entertainment skills—she had been channeled into a low-level government job from which neither her intelligence nor her competence would ever elevate her. But her other government-designated career track had been D-3 Convenience Prostitute, and only the the shortage of PCOs caused by the higher suicide rate in the D-3 Pact Covenant Observer career field had saved her from that fate. The people she had to watch burn themselves to death on People's Home of Truth and Fairness worlds haunted her. The executions she had to certify haunted her. She didn't question for an instant the reason D-3 PCOs had the highest suicide rate of any career field in the Pact Worlds.

Her plan was to disappear from her job before it devoured her, too.

In front of her, left-side Suzee said, "Because I am guilty of five murders of men designated A-1, and because I freely confess that I committed these murders by intent..."

Right-side Suzee also said, "Because I am guilty of five murders of men designated A-1, and because I freely confess that I committed these murders by intent..."

Left-side and right-side Suzees both said, "I waive my right to trial in order to save the Pact Worlds the cost of such trial when the outcome is already certain, and instead elect to sell my death to the highest-bidding Death Circus, where my execution will be streamed for all viewers on all Pact Worlds. All Pact Worlds citizens need to be able to see me receiving the consequences of my actions."

Charlie didn't the hear Suzee's last few words, however.

She was out the door and shooting herself onto the *Longview's* passenger bridge transport, screaming, "I need to speak to the owner, I need to speak to the owner now!"

Shay, the owner's representative, was on the bridge waiting for her when the passenger transport unlocked.

"Suzee Delight is selling herself to the highest-bidding Death Circus now," Charlie shouted.

Both the captain and first mate looked back at the two of them.

Shay looked startled, then pleased. "Oh, that's excellent. You and I will go to the owner's quarters, Charlie. His condition is bothering him again, so he won't meet with you personally, but you and I will talk, and he'll watch us and relay suggestions to me." She paused. "I'm assuming that you've brought this to me because you hope the owner will buy Suzee Delight's execution."

"Of course."

"Because you want to be the one to witness it?"

Shay's suggestion was as far from Charlie's truth as it was possible to get.

But Charlie shrugged and nodded. "That... is as good an explanation as any."

The corners of Shay's mouth twitched. "You have good entrepreneurial instincts. Come with me, then. I'll let the owner know we have an investment opportunity for him."

TALES FROM THE LONGVIEW: EPISODE 2—The Selling of Suzee Delight is available now.

CHAPTER 2

Charlie

Charlie, the *Longview's* Mandatory Pact Covenant Observer, sat in Passenger Room 5, her *Longview* quarters, and on split screens watched what was being billed as the holocast of the century, presented by ever-smiling Danyal Travers, who had been covering the story for days. Each of Charlie's two screens showed a different datastream of the same event.

On the left screen, she had the official Pact Worlds coverage of the public confession and sentencing of Suzee Delight, First Courtesan of the Diamond Dome, superstar goddess of a thousand Sensos—some actually suitable for general audiences—and reputed simultaneous murderer of the Administrators of the five most important Pact Worlds.

On the right screen, she had the raw, siphoned, underground version of the same feed. If Charlie's Pact Worlds controller ever discovered that she watched unofficial feeds of anything streamed from the Pact Worlds, he would recall her and drop her citizenship level to F-10: Permanently Unemployable, Sentenced to Minimal Survival Assistance Only.

However, as long as she was assigned to the *Longview* and had Passenger Room 5 to herself, she was safe. If she did her job and made sure the Pact Worlds received a steady stream of money in exchange for their sentenced criminals, she could hope to remain aboard the *Longview*, where she was treated better than she'd ever been treated in her life, for at least a couple more years before she received mandatory rotation orders.

Charlie's only objective where her controller was concerned was to remain unremarkable—to do an average job, turn in average numbers, and in all ways be an invisible cog in the Pact Worlds' massive machine.

So she was content that the *Longview*, rumored to be the most profitable Death Circus franchise in Settled Space for its owner, only managed to stay in the middle of the pack where its profits on criminals bought and sold was concerned. How its owner made his *other* money was officially none of her concern.

Unofficially...

...Well, anything she knew, she might be able to use to her own benefit. And she'd made it her business to know a lot.

Until she found a way to use what she knew, Charlie had decided that if she received rotation or recall orders, she planned to defect. Her defection details were fuzzy, but she was getting them together.

Meanwhile, however, she was in a position to make a difference for people the Pact Worlds considered fodder.

So she watched, tense, anxious, and at the same time hopeful.

Left-side Suzee said, "I am ashamed of my actions. I betrayed the trust of five men I loved, and used my position of trust to murder them because I envied them their power."

Right-side Suzee said, "I am not ashamed of my actions. These five men betrayed the people they served. They planned to use their positions of trust and power to destroy the autonomy of the citizens they claim to represent."

The cutwork on the official version had been skillfully done. Charlie couldn't see or hear the blending between the segments that were actually Suzee's words, and those that had been inserted.

Most of Settled Space would see the raw version, would know the venom in Travers' voice as he asked her the questions, would see his eyes glitter as he envisioned her eventual fate.

Most citizens of the Pact Worlds, however, would only have access to the official version, which had little truth in it.

Left-side Suzee said, "I failed my government, my educators, my selectors, my trainers, my clients, and my profession as a courtesan—the highest calling to which any woman can aspire."

Right-side Suzee said, "I accuse my government, my educators, my selectors, my trainers, and my clients for creating laws that make being a courtesan the highest work to which any woman can aspire."

"Damned right," Charlie muttered. "You tell 'em, Suzee."

Charlie had been lucky enough to be born homely and lacking in any discernible entertainment skills—she had been channeled into a low-level government job from which neither her intelligence nor her competence would ever elevate her. But her other government-designated career track had been D-3 Convenience Prostitute, and only the the shortage of PCOs caused by the higher suicide rate in the D-3 Pact Covenant Observer career field had saved her from that fate. The people she had to watch burn themselves to death on People's Home of Truth and Fairness worlds haunted her. The executions she had to certify haunted her. She didn't question for an instant the reason D-3 PCOs had the highest suicide rate of any career field in the Pact Worlds.

Her plan was to disappear from her job before it devoured her, too.

In front of her, left-side Suzee said, "Because I am guilty of five murders of men designated A-1, and because I freely confess that I committed these murders by intent..."

Right-side Suzee also said, "Because I am guilty of five murders of men designated A-1, and because I freely confess that I committed these murders by intent..."

Left-side and right-side Suzees both said, "I waive my right to trial in order to save the Pact Worlds the cost of such trial when the outcome is already certain, and instead elect to sell my death to the highest-bidding Death Circus, where my execution will be streamed for all viewers on all Pact Worlds. All Pact Worlds citizens need to be able to see me receiving the consequences of my actions."

Charlie didn't the hear Suzee's last few words, however.

She was out the door and shooting herself onto the *Longview's* passenger bridge transport, screaming, "I need to speak to the owner, I need to speak to the owner now!"

Shay, the owner's representative, was on the bridge waiting for her when the passenger transport unlocked.

"Suzee Delight is selling herself to the highest-bidding Death Circus now," Charlie shouted.

Both the captain and first mate looked back at the two of them.

Shay looked startled, then pleased. "Oh, that's excellent. You and I will go to the owner's quarters, Charlie. His condition is bothering him again, so he won't meet with you personally, but you and I will talk, and he'll watch us and relay suggestions to me." She paused. "I'm assuming that you've brought this to me because you hope the owner will buy Suzee Delight's execution."

"Of course."

"Because you want to be the one to witness it?"

Shay's suggestion was as far from Charlie's truth as it was possible to get.

But Charlie shrugged and nodded. "That... is as good an explanation as any."

The corners of Shay's mouth twitched. "You have good entrepreneurial instincts. Come with me, then. I'll let the owner know we have an investment opportunity for him."

Suzee Delight

I'm locked inside a large Senso recording studio with four moleibond walls, a moleibond ceiling, and a moleibond floor. My captors are recording every instant of my captivity, and are selling the feed at several price-points, the least expensive being "Suitable for all viewers," and the most expensive, which does not include any blurring or decency shielding, and which does include full-Senso connectivity, being "Live Suzee Delight's Last Days: Credit Rating A and above only."

My cell contains a luxurious transparent bathtub and non-bubbling body wash; a Nestor Insta-Dress wardrobe programmed to instantly create any of thousands of exotic costumes for me—all of them see-through; a silk-sheeted bed; my musical instruments and art supplies and the necessary equipment to use them; a transparent dining table and chair; a small but elegant reconsta unit with Bailey's Irish Reconsta—because the Senso viewers would complain and rate the Senso badly if they had to taste sub-par reconsta while living inside my skin with me—and a set of specific instructions on what I am to do with myself while I wait to be sold.

Before I was locked in my cell, my final Pleasure Master told me exactly what will happen to me while I'm waiting if I do not obey that list. It will not be pleasant, but there are certain Senso buyers who will pay a premium for the experience, should I decide to indulge them by being disobedient.

They are not the buyers I ever hope to entertain.

So I am still doing the work I hate. Making prison Sensos for Suzee Delight fans—and making one last fortune for the Pact Worlds.

Because it amuses the Pleasure Masters who have caged me to let me know how much money the Pact Worlds are making from my imprisonment and will make from my execution, they've placed a sales board for the feed and Senso on the control corridor. I can always see it, but the viewers and Senso fans cannot. To people looking at my world through my eyes, it will be edited to read as a pretty wall.

Three hours after the Death Circus bidding opened, my imprisonment recordings are already outselling everything else I've ever done.

It hurts me that the same people who claimed to love me are leaping at the opportunity to indulge in my destruction.

I entertain them as I've been told to do, and I watch the boards.

The Death Circus bidding has already started, too—three hours in, low bids from small Death Circuses I've never heard of have given way to bigger and more profitable circuses.

The name of the ship I'm hoping to see has not yet flashed across the board, though. Three hours in, twenty ships have dropped out of a field of over a hundred. His ship is not among them—and wasn't even in the showing early on.

He told me his ship was a successful Death Circus, but I have no idea how successful. Perhaps it will not be able to afford to bid on me.

He told me if I ever found a need to escape, he would find his way to me. And maybe he meant that, but something is standing in his way.

Unlike many of my clients, he never made a pretense of love. But he expressed great admiration for my skill and intelligence. Perhaps he was only being kind.

Perhaps—like the words of so many others—his words had nothing behind them.

Perhaps he wasn't as important or powerful as he claimed to be, and now that I had put myself in his hands, they were tied, and he could do nothing to get his ship to me.

Perhaps I believed him simply because he never hurt me.

And perhaps I'll never know the truth.

I murdered the five chief Pact Worlds Administrators because it was the right thing to do. I do not regret it.

But in the back of my mind, I held as my private reward the promise that I would escape punishment for my crime.

And perhaps—like every other part of my life but one—this last piece of my existence will betray me.

ACKNOWLEDGMENTS

I want to take a moment to thank my Patreon patrons, whose encouragement, readership, faith in me, and funding have made it possible for me to get back to writing fiction every weekday.

Hero Patrons

Julian Adorney, Thomas Vetter, Tuff Gartin, Karin Hernandez, Nancy Nielsen-Brown, Holly Doyne, Katharina Gerlach, Kim Lambert, John Toppins, Rebecca Yeo, Rebecca Galardo, Eva Gorup, Dragonwing, Isabella Leigh, Misti Pyles, Susan Qrose, Tammi Labrecque, Kirsten Bolda, Patricia Masserman, Charlotte Babb, KM Nalle, Benita Peters, Michelle Miles, Becky Sasala, Joyce Sully, Jean Schara, Carolyn Stein, Dan Allen, Heiko Ludwig, Renee Wittman, Dawn Morrison, Christine Embree, Justin Colucci, Angelika Devlyn, Mary E. Merrell, Indy Indie, Moley, Tiny Yellow Tree, Brendan Fortune, Greg Miranda, Wednesday McKenna, Nicola Lane, Jane Lawson, Michelle Mulford, Julie Hickerson, Amy Fahrer, Jess,

Juneta Key, Lynda Washington, Reetta Raitanen, Marya Miller, Faith Nelson, Meagan Smith, Sarah Brewe, Ava Fairhall, Elke Zimoch, Zeyana Musthafa, Beverly Paty, Misty DiFrancesco, Nan Sampson, Eric Bateman, Bonnie Burns, Maureen Morley, Resa Edwards, Jennette Heikes, Sylvie Granville, Miriam Stark, Anders Bruce, Paula Meengs, Alexandra Swanson, Claudia Wickstrom, Ken Bristow, Francine Seal, Amy Padgett, Jason Anderson, Doug Glassford

Amazing Patrons

Felicia Fredlund, Susan Osthaus, Hope Terrell, Glenwood Bretz, Amy Schaffer, Deb Gallardo, Anna Bunce, Simon Sawyers, Deb Evon, Ernesto Montalve, Teresa Horne, Erin O'Kelly, Cynthia Louise Adams, June Thornton, Cassie Witt, Liza Olmsted, Elaine S. Milner, Kristen Shields, Alex G. Zarate, Barbara Lund, Cathy Peper, Ken Alger, Donna Mann, Linda George

Wonderful Patrons

Irina Barnay, Peggy Elam, Chris Muir, Ewelina Sparks, Betty Widerski, Stacie Arellano, Elizabeth Schroeder, Kara Hash, Amber Hansford, Beverley Spindler, Daniela Gana, Thea van Diepen, Storm Weaver, Susanne, Panos, Pixelkay, Ruth Sard, Dori-Ann Granger, Connie Cockrell

Want to find out more about becoming a fiction patron?

Start Here: https://www.patreon.com/hollylisle

ABOUT THE AUTHOR

I'm a commercial novelist who went indie.

Lots of reasons, all good but none easy. In July of 2011 I walked away from commercial publishing to pursue *My Career My Way,* and it's been interesting times ever since.

Holly Lisle

Now I'm back to writing the *Cadence Drake, Moon & Sun,* and *Longview* series, creating stand-alone fiction, building writing courses, and getting the chance to speak directly to the readers of both my fiction and nonfiction.

If you keep hoping I'll do a particular story, or book, or course, and I haven't yet—let me know.

Cheerfully,
Holly Lisle

P.S. To find out what's coming next, and let me know what you'd love to see next...

Join Holly's SF & Fantasy Readers for free
https://hollyswritingclasses.com/go/get-free-sff-stories.html

ALSO BY HOLLY LISLE

Settled Space & Cadence Drake Stories

Tales from the Longview: Episode 1 - Born from Fire
Tales from the Longview: Episode 2 - The Selling of Suzee Delight
Tales from the Longview: Episode 3 - The Philosopher Gambit
Tales from the Longview: Episode 4 - Gunslinger Moon
Tales from the Longview: Episode 5 - The Vipers' Nest
Hunting the Corrigan's Blood
Warpaint
The Wishbone Conspiracy (coming soon)

My Other Novels

The Ruby Key: Moon & Sun I
The Silver Door: Moon & Sun II
Talyn: A Novel of Korre
Hawkspar: A Novel of Korre
Midnight Rain
Last Girl Dancing
I See You
Night Echoes

Fire in the Mist: Arhel I

Bones of the Past: Arhel II

Mind of the Magic: Arhel III

Sympathy for the Devil: Devil's Point I

The Devil and Dan Cooley (with Walter Spence): Devil's Point II

Hell on High (with Ted Nolan): Devil's Point III

Minerva Wakes

Memory of Fire: World Gates I

The Wreck of Heaven: World Gates II

Gods Old and Dark: World Gates III

Diplomacy of Wolves: Secret Texts I

Vengeance of Dragons: Secret Texts II

Courage of Falcons: Secret Texts III

Vincalis the Agitator (Secret Texts Prequel)

Glenraven (with Marion Zimmer Bradley)

In The Rift: Glenraven II (with Marion Zimmer Bradley)

When the Bough Breaks (with Mercedes Lackey)

Mall, Mayhem and Magic (with Chris Guin)

The Rose Sea (with S.M.Stirling)

Curse of the Black Heron

Thunder of the Captains (with Aaron Allston)

Wrath of the Princes (with Aaron Allston)

My Singles (stand-alone short fiction)

Light Through Fog

Rewind

Strange Arrivals: Ten Tiny, Twisty Fantasy Tales

My Stories in Collections

"Light Through Fog," The Mammoth Book of Paranormal Romance

"4EVR," The Mammoth Book of Ghost Romance

"Last Thorsday Night," The Mammoth Book of Time Travel

"Knight and the Enemy," The Enchanter Reborn

"Armor-ella," Chicks in Chainmail

"A Few Good Men," Women at War

My Nonfiction

Create A World Clinic: A Step-by-Step Course for the Fiction Writer

Create A Plot Clinic: A Step-by-Step Course for the Fiction Writer

Create A Culture Clinic: A Step-by-Step Course for the Fiction Writer

Create A Language Clinic: A Step-by-Step Course for the Fiction Writer

Create A Character Clinic: A Step-by-Step Course for the Fiction Writer

How to Write Page-Turning Scenes: A Step-by-Step Course for the Fiction Writer

Mugging the Muse: Writing Fiction for Love AND Money

Professional Plot Outline

Nonfiction Site Exclusives

(These courses are ONLY available on
HollysWritingClasses.com)

How to Write Flash Fiction that Doesn't SUCK: A Free Three-Week Course for Everyone

How to Think Sideways: Career Survival School for Writers
(seven-month writing course)

How to Revise Your Novel: Get the Book You Want from the Wreck You Wrote (five-month revision course)

How to Write A Series: Master the Art of Sequential Fiction

Title. Cover. Copy. - Fiction Marketing Workshop

7-Day Crash Revision: How to Do the Clean-Up Revision of an Entire Novel in One (Desperate) Week

(7-Day Workshop, also works with short fiction and self-publishing)

How to Find Your Writing Discipline (3-Day Workshop)

21 Ways to Get Yourself Writing When Your Life Has Just Exploded (Workshop)

How to Write Dialogue with Subtext: Give Your Characters Conversations that MATTER (Workshop)

How to Motivate Yourself: Discover Your Hidden Triggers and Barriers and Use BOTH to Get Writing (Workshop)